Usborne English Readers

Starter Level

# THE BAOBAB TREE

Retold by Laura Cowan

Illustrated by Jesús López

English language consultant: Peter Viney

# Contents

*⟨⟨⟨*

You can listen to the story online here:
usborneenglishreaders.com/
baobabtree

This is a story about the beginning of the world. There is nothing in it. The gods make everything. They make the land and the sea and the sky.

They make the animals on the land.
They make the fish in the sea, and the
birds in the sky. They make flowers
and leaves and trees, too.

The first tree is a talking tree.
Its name is the Baobab tree.

The gods love the Baobab tree.
They give it sun. They send it rain,
but the tree isn't happy. The Baobab
tree doesn't like *anything*. The Baobab
tree complains about *everything*.

"I don't like this sun," complains
the tree, "It's really hot. It's hurting
my leaves."

"I don't like this rain,"
complains the tree.
"It's really wet.
My roots are cold."

After the rain, the gods send wind.
"Oh, I don't like this wind,"
complains the tree.

Now I'm
REALLY cold!

When birds sit on the Baobab tree, the tree complains. "Ow, that's hurting my leaves!"

When animals make holes under the Baobab tree, the tree complains. "Ow, that's hurting my roots!" The animals and birds don't go near the Baobab tree after that.

The gods make more trees. They
make a tree with very long leaves.
The animals sit under the tree, out
of the sun. The Baobab tree sees the
new tree and it is *not* happy.

The gods hear the Baobab tree.
They can *always* hear the Baobab tree.
"That tree!" they say, "It complains
all the time. It never stops!"

Look at
those leaves!

They are
really nice
and long.

Mine are
short!

The gods make more trees. Some have beautiful flowers, red and purple flowers. The Baobab tree sees the new trees and their beautiful flowers. "Where are *my* flowers? *I* don't have flowers," complains the tree.

*I* want beautiful flowers, too.

The gods hear the Baobab tree and they are angry. They come down to the land and talk to the tree.

"Listen to us! Stop complaining," they say.

"What do you mean?" complains the Baobab tree. "I never complain."

The gods make more trees with beautiful fruit, orange, red and purple fruit. The birds and animals eat the fruit and they are happy.

"Where is my fruit?" complains the Baobab tree, "*I* would like fruit. Fruit is good. Everyone likes fruit. They don't like me!"

So the gods give the Baobab tree some fruit, too

"No! I don't like my fruit," says the Baobab tree.

It's green and ugly. I want nice fruit!

The gods are really angry now. They come down to the land again.

"*Stop complaining!*" they say. "We give you everything and you never say thank you."

"You give me *nothing*," says the Baobab tree. "I don't have flowers. My fruit is ugly, and look at my leaves!"

"*That's it,*" the gods say. They make a big hole, then they pick up the Baobab tree. They put its head and its leaves in the hole. Its roots are in the sky now.

The Baobab tree doesn't say anything. It can't... and it never says *anything* again.

# The Baobab Tree in real life

The Baobab Tree is a real tree. It grows in Africa.

Baobab trees can grow for hundreds of years.

Real Baobab trees have pink, yellow or white flowers.

They have large green fruit.

People cook and eat the leaves, and eat the fruit too.

What kinds of trees grow near you?
Do they have flowers and fruit?

# Activities

The answers are on page 32.

## Can you see it in the picture?
### Which three things *can't* you see?

animal  bird  face  fish  flower  gods
leaves  road  roots  sky  tree  water

# I never complain

## Which of these sentences are true?

1. The Baobab tree never says thank you.
2. The Baobab tree never complains.
3. The Baobab tree has beautiful flowers.
4. The Baobab tree has short leaves.

# What do the gods make?

Choose the right words for each picture.

  1. A talking tree.
  2. A tree with very long leaves.
  3. The land and the sea and the sky.
  4. A quiet tree, now.

A.
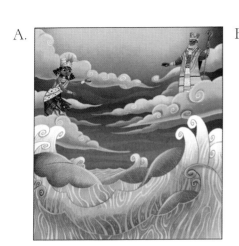

B.

C.

D.

# What are they thinking?

## Match the words to the pictures.

Stop complaining!

That's hurting my roots!

I want nice fruit!

We like this tree.

1.

2.

3.

4.

# Stop complaining!

Choose the right word for each sentence.

> beautiful   cold   happy   hot
> hungry   sad   short   wet

1.

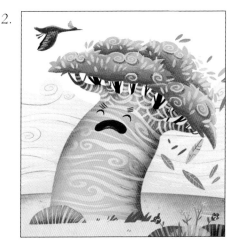

"This rain's really ........!"

2.

"I'm REALLY ........!"

3.

"My leaves are ........!"

4.

"I want ........ flowers too!"

# Word list

**after** (adv) later in time than something else.

**beginning** (n) the start of something.

**complain** (v) when you are not happy about something and you say so, you complain.

**first** (adj) before the others or before anything else.

**fruit** (n) fruit grows on trees. You can eat fruit. Apples are a kind of fruit.

**god** (n) in stories, gods are very strong. They can live forever and do magic.

**hole** (n) an empty space, or the space you make when you take something away.

sky

gods

**land** (n) the part of the world where animals and people live.

**leaves** (n pl) leaves are usually green, and grow on plants or trees.

**roots** (n pl) the part of a plant or tree that grows under the ground.

**sky** (n) the sky is above us. The sun and the stars are in the sky.

**ugly** (adj) when something is ugly, it doesn't look nice, it looks bad.

**wind** (n) a kind of weather. Wind is air moving quickly.

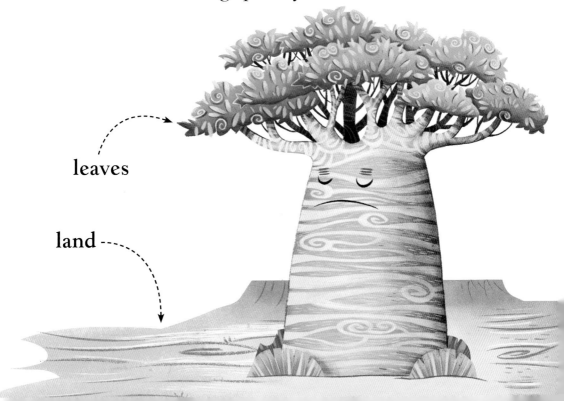

leaves

land

# Answers

**Can you see it in the picture?**

Three things you can't see: gods, road, roots.

**I never complain**

Sentences 1 and 4 are true.

**What do the gods make?**

1. B  2. C  3. A  4. D

**What are they thinking?**

Stop complaining! 4
That's hurting my roots! 1
I want nice fruit! 3
We like this tree. 2

**Stop complaining!**

1. wet
2. cold
3. short
4. beautiful

 You can find information about other Usborne English Readers here: usborneenglishreaders.com

Designed by Vickie Robinson
Series designer: Laura Nelson Norris
Edited by Mairi Mackinnon

First published in 2021 by Usborne Publishing Ltd.,
Usborne House, 83-85 Saffron Hill, London EC1N 8RT, England.
www.usborne.com Copyright © 2021 Usborne Publishing Ltd.